Welcome to ALADDIN QUIX!

If you are looking for fast, fun-to-read stories with colorful characters, lots of kid-friendly humor, easy-to-follow action, entertaining story lines, and lively illustrations, then **ALADDIN QUIX** is for you!

But wait, there's more!

If you're also looking for stories with tables of contents; word lists; about-the-book questions; 64, 80, or 96 pages; short chapters; short paragraphs; and large fonts, then **ALADDIN QUIX** is *definitely* for you!

ALADDIN QUIX: The next step between ready to reads and longer, more challenging chapter books, for readers five to eight years old.

Read more ALADDIN QUIX books!

Mack Rhino, Private Eye
By Paul DuBois Jacobs and Jennifer Swender

Book 1: *The Big Race Lace Case*

Book 2: *The Candy Caper Case*

By Stephanie Calmenson

Our Principal Is a Frog!

Our Principal Is a Wolf!

Our Principal's in His Underwear!

Our Principal Breaks a Spell!

A Miss Mallard Mystery
By Robert Quackenbush

Dig to Disaster

Texas Trail to Calamity

Express Train to Trouble

Stairway to Doom

Bicycle to Treachery

Gondola to Danger

Surfboard to Peril

Taxi to Intrigue

Cable Car to Catastrophe

Little Goddess Girls
By Joan Holub and Suzanne Williams

Book 1: *Athena & the Magic Land*

Book 2: *Persephone & the Giant Flowers*

Book 3: *Aphrodite & the Gold Apple*

MACK RHINO
PRIVATE EYE'

The Unfair Fair Case

BY
PAUL DUBOIS JACOBS
AND JENNIFER SWENDER

ILLUSTRATED BY KARL WEST

ALADDIN QUIX

New York London Toronto Sydney New Delhi

For our favorite clowns—
Littles and Chico

ALADDIN QUIX
Simon & Schuster Children's Publishing Division
1230 Avenue of the Americas, New York, New York 10020
First Aladdin QUIX paperback edition September 2021
Text copyright © 2021 by Jennifer Swender and Paul DuBois Jacobs
Illustrations copyright © 2021 by Karl West
Also available in an Aladdin QUIX hardcover edition.
All rights reserved, including the right of reproduction in whole or in part in any form.
ALADDIN and the related marks and colophon are trademarks of
Simon & Schuster, Inc.
For information about special discounts for bulk purchases, please contact
Simon & Schuster Special Sales at 1-866-506-1949 or business@simonandschuster.com.
The Simon & Schuster Speakers Bureau can bring authors to your live event. For more information or to book an event contact the Simon & Schuster Speakers Bureau at
1-866-248-3049 or visit our website at www.simonspeakers.com.
Designed by Tiara Iandiorio
The illustrations for this book were rendered digitally.
The text of this book was set in Archer Medium.
Manufactured in the United States of America 0821 OFF
2 4 6 8 10 9 7 5 3 1
Library of Congress Control Number 2021940843
ISBN 978-1-5344-7997-5 (hc)
ISBN 978-1-5344-7996-8 (pbk)
ISBN 978-1-5344-7998-2 (ebook)

Cast of Characters

Mack Rhino, Private Eye: a detective

Redd Oxpeck: Mack's trusted assistant

Al Gator: director of the Coral Cove Fair

Surfer Jo: a local surfer at the fair

Lifeguard Sally: a local lifeguard at the fair

Juggling Jenkins Twins: two kids performing at the fair

Octavia Octopus: a fairgoer who is winning all the games

A small fry: a young fairgoer

Terry Berry: Mack and Redd's friend; owner of the Smoothie Cart

Bobbi Boa: a fair worker running the Bowling Game

Contents

That's the Ticket!

Snug in his office at Number 21 Beach Street, **Mack Rhino, Private Eye**, rolled up the blinds and rolled up his sleeves.

For cases big or small, Mack Rhino, Private Eye, was your guy.

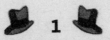

Or . . . rhino.

Mack poured himself a mug of chocolate milk. He took out his notebook. He reviewed his list.

Hat √
Sunscreen √
Tickets?

"Now, where did I put those tickets?" he said.

Mack searched his desk.

He searched the floor.

"What are you looking for?"

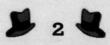

asked **Redd Oxpeck**, his trusted assistant.

"Our tickets to the Coral Cove Fair," said Mack. **"I can't find them anywhere."**

"Goodness!" said Redd. "Let me help you look for them."

Mack and Redd loved the Coral Cove Fair. They loved the rides and treats. They loved the games and prizes. Redd especially loved the fun house. **It was his favorite!**

Mack took out his notebook.

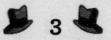 3

He added this to his list:

Find those tickets!

Despite the missing tickets, Mack was in a good mood. He and Redd had just solved their 101st case.

Case #101—The Candy Caper Case—was a sticky situation. False alarms kept Mack and Redd running up and down Beach Street, but they soon unwrapped the sneaky plot.

Crafty cat burglars were stealing valuables and replacing them with candy copies. Good thing Mack had a keen nose for chocolate. He and Redd managed to lick the case (and the candy) just in time.

It was a sweet success!

Something Fishy

"Hey, Boss," said Redd. **"Take a look at this!"**

Redd held up the morning newspaper. He pointed to the headline. "Opening day is already sold out!" he said.

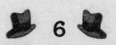

"We'd better find those tickets," said Mack.

"They're probably right under your horn." Redd giggled.

But before Mack and Redd

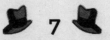

could continue their search—

Ring-ring. Ring-ring.

Mack answered the phone. "Mack Rhino, Private Eye. For cases big or small, I'm your guy. Or . . . rhino."

Mack heard a *whoosh*.

He heard a *ding*!

He heard music.

Was it **carousel** music?

"Hi, Mack," said a voice. "It's **Al Gator**, director of the Coral Cove Fair."

"Hi there, Al," said Mack.

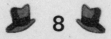

"We were just looking for our tickets."

"Don't worry about tickets," said Al. **"I need your help!"**

"What seems to be the trouble?" asked Mack.

"There's something fishy at the fair," said Al. "I hope you can get to the bottom of it."

"We'll be there in a **jiffy**!" said Mack.

He hung up the phone.

"What is it, Boss?" asked Redd.

"That was Al Gator," said Mack.

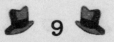

"Grab your camera. We're going to the fair!"

Mack tucked his notebook into his pocket. He picked up his magnifying glass.

"But we still haven't found our tickets," said Redd.

"No need for tickets," said Mack. **"This is the start of Case #102!"**

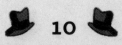

Fair and Square

Mack and Redd hurried over to the Coral Cove Fair.

Al Gator met them at the front gate and **ushered** them through.

The *Beach Street Gazette* had been right about the crowds. The

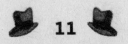

fairgrounds were packed **to the gills.**

Mack spotted the usual faces—**Surfer Jo**, **Lifeguard Sally**, and the **Juggling Jenkins Twins**.

He also spotted the usual places—the Photo Booth of Make-Believe, Amusement Alley, the fun house, and the Snack Barn.

"Thanks for coming so quickly," said Al. **"I'm in quite a pickle."**

"What seems to be the problem?" asked Mack.

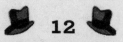 12

"We have a slippery situation," said Al.

"Slippery?" asked Redd.

"An octopus named **Octavia** is

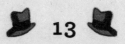

winning every game in Amusement Alley," Al explained.

"Every game?" said Mack. **"What are the chances?"**

"I don't know how she's doing it," said Al. "What's more, she's collecting all the prizes."

"That doesn't seem fair," said Redd.

"The fairgoers are starting to get **frustrated**," said Al. "I've tried to speak with Octavia, but she's always one step ahead of me."

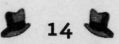

"Is that so?" asked Mack.

Just then Al's walkie-talkie crackled. "Al," a voice called. "You're needed in the Snack Barn."

"Be right there," Al said into the walkie-talkie.

"And when you're finished there," crackled the voice, "they need you at the front gate."

"Got it," said Al. He turned to Mack and Redd. "I have to run. I sure could use an extra set of hands around here. Please

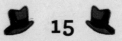 15

let me know what you find."

"Will do," said Mack.

Mack took out his notebook. He jotted down a few questions.

> How is Octavia winning every game?
>
> Is she playing fair and square?

"Time to put this fair back on track," said Mack. "Next stop . . ."

"Amusement Alley?" asked Redd.

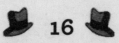 16

"Soon," said Mack. "First, let's swing by the Photo Booth of Make-Believe."

"Is now really the time for

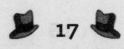 17

photos, Boss?" asked Redd.

"Not photos," whispered Mack. "Disguises. We need to blend in. We are going undercover."

Fair Play

A few minutes later, two clowns **emerged** from the Photo Booth of Make-Believe.

One jumbo. One mini.

They had round, red noses.

They had curly, colorful wigs.

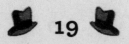

They had funny, floppy shoes.

One held a notebook. One held a camera.

"Mr. Clown! Mr. Clown!" called a **small fry**. "Can you make a balloon animal for me, please?"

"Coming right up," said Mack.

But try as he might, Mack popped every balloon. His horn kept getting in the way.

"Hey, Boss, can I lend you a hand . . . or wing?" asked Redd, smiling.

With a few expert twists, Redd

unveiled a purple puppy dog.

The small fry jumped up and down with excitement. **"Thank you! Thank you!"**

"Where did you learn how to do that?" Mack asked Redd.

"Clown school, of course," said Redd with a wink.

Mack and Redd continued on to Amusement Alley.

Mack scanned the crowd.

Surfer Jo was in the dunk tank.

Lifeguard Sally was at the giant ring toss.

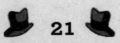

And the Juggling Jenkins Twins were putting on quite a show.

Then Mack spotted an eight-legged fairgoer pulling a wagon overflowing with prizes.

"That must be Octavia," he whispered.

Mack and Redd watched as she smoothly glided over to the popular dart-and-balloon booth. They watched as she threw eight darts.

Pop! Pop! Pop! Pop! Pop! Pop! Pop! Pop!

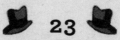

Every single dart popped a
balloon.

Mack took out his notebook. He
jotted down a few questions.

Is it luck?

Is it skill?

Does she have a
trick up her sleeve?

Pop! *Pop!* **Pop!** *Pop!*
Pop! *Pop!* **Pop!** *Pop!*

Again, Octavia popped every
balloon.

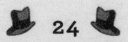

One by one, the other players walked away **deflated**.

Octavia kept right on winning until the booth was flat out of balloons. Then she loaded all the prizes into her wagon and slipped away into the crowd.

"Follow that **cephalopod**!" cried Redd.

"Ceph-a-lo-*what*?" asked Mack.

"It's a fancy name for an octopus, Boss," said Redd.

"Where did you learn that?" asked Mack.

"Clown school," said Redd with a wink.

A Smoothie Operator

Octavia surfaced near the bumper cars. She wove her way past the Ferris wheel, round and around the carousel, and into the Snack Barn. Mack and Redd stayed close on her heels . . . or arms.

Inside the Snack Barn, Octavia **beelined** straight for **Terry Berry**'s Smoothie Cart.

This was a lucky break. Mack needed to think, and it just so happened he did his best thinking with a Terry Berry smoothie.

Mack and Redd listened in as Octavia politely asked for a Malted Mollusk.

They watched as she brought her smoothie and her wagon of prizes over to a picnic table.

They observed that she sat all by herself.

Mack took out his notebook. He jotted down a few more notes.

No sidekick.

No partner in crime.

Is she a lone wolf?

It was now Mack and Redd's turn to order.

"Hello," said Terry. "What can I get for you?"

"We'll have the usual," said Mack.

"I'm sorry, Mr. Clown," said Terry. "I'm afraid I don't know what your usual is."

Mack leaned in close. **"Psst,"** he whispered. **"Terry, it's us!"**

"Mack and Redd?" asked Terry. "I didn't recognize you guys. Why are you dressed like clowns?"

"We're undercover," whispered Redd.

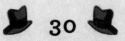 30

"Then, two Banana Supremes, coming right up," said Terry. She poured the smoothies and popped a lid onto each cup. "And now your smoothies are undercover too."

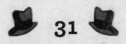

The next customer stepped up to the Smoothie Cart. He was a very blue whale.

"What can I get for you?" asked Terry.

"Do you have any smoothies left?" the whale asked **glumly**.

"Of course," said Terry. **"Why do you ask?"**

"Well, they've run out of prizes at the giant ring toss, the coin toss, *and* the beanbag toss. I might as well toss in the towel."

"Run out of prizes?" asked Terry.

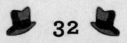

"The same thing happened at the Ping-Pong toss," said a flamingo who was next in line. **"It's that Octavia Octopus.** She's got a leg up on everybody."

"Eight legs, to be exact," said Redd.

"Well, she's spoiling the fair for the rest of us," said the whale.

"Not to worry," Mack assured him. "I'm sure

the fair is keeping an eye on it."

"A private eye," said Redd.

But when Mack and Redd looked over to the picnic table, Octavia and her wagon of prizes were nowhere to be seen.

Where had she slipped off to now?

Pick a Prize

Mack and Redd jumped into action.

"Let's split up," said Mack. "That way we can cover more ground."

"You mean *fair*ground," said Redd.

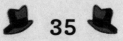

Mack made his way through the crowd. Redd flew high in the sky.

"I see her, Boss!" Redd called. "She's heading to **Bobbi Boa**'s Bowling Game."

"Perfect," said Mack.

It just so happened that Mack Rhino was an expert bowler. He and Redd bowled every Friday night at the Coral Cove Bowling Alley.

"Here's our chance to see if Octavia is playing fair and square," said Mack.

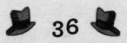

36

"Good thinking," said Redd. "And while you bowl, I'll snap photos with my camera. Maybe we can catch her red-handed."

Mack and Redd zipped over to the booth.

"Step right up! Step right up!" called Bobbi Boa. "We need at least two to play!"

Octavia was the only player there.

Mack stepped forward and raised his hand. "I'll give it a try," he said.

"We have a challenger!" announced Bobbi. She handed Mack a ball. "Now, no clowning around, okay?" she said, and smiled.

Mack nodded. He carefully took aim. He bowled.

But his large clown nose got in the way.

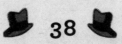 38

"Seven pins!" called Bobbi.

"Drat," said Mack.

Next it was Octavia's turn. Bobbi handed her the ball.

Redd got his camera into position.

Octavia took aim.

Redd snapped a photo. *Click!*

Octavia released the ball.

CLICK

Redd snapped another photo. *Click!*

Octavia bowled a perfect strike. *Click! Click!*

"We have a winner!" called Bobbi. "Pick a prize."

"I'd like the green gorilla, please," said Octavia in a voice as soft as a whisper.

"Here you go," said Bobbi. "Care to play again?"

"Yes, please," said Octavia.

"And how about you, Mr. Clown?" asked Bobbi.

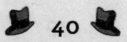

"Count me in," said Mack.

A crowd started to gather around the booth.

Mack **adjusted** his clown nose. He picked up the ball. He took aim.

But this time his curly clown wig got in the way.

"Six pins!" called Bobbi.

"Double drat," said Mack.

It was Octavia's turn again. She took aim.

Redd snapped a photo. *Click!*

Octavia smoothly released the ball.

Click! Click!

"Another strike!" called Bobbi. "What are the chances? Pick a prize."

"I'd like the glow-in-the-dark

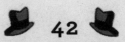

space creature, please," Octavia said softly.

"Here you go," said Bobbi. "Care to play again?"

"Yes, please," said Octavia.

"Sure thing," said Mack.

"You can do it, Boss," whispered Redd.

The crowd grew larger.

Mack adjusted his clown wig. He picked up the ball. He took aim.

But this time he stumbled over his floppy clown shoes.

"Five pins!" called Bobbi.

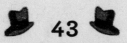 43

"**Jeepers,**" said Mack. He felt defeated.

Just then, the small fry from earlier popped out of the crowd.

"I would like to play too," he said. **"I really want to win that giraffe!"** He excitedly pointed to a giant giraffe displayed above the pins.

"Well, step right up," said Bobbi. "Let's see what you can do."

The small fry handed his balloon animal to his dad. Then he picked up the ball. He took a deep

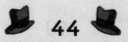

breath. He took aim and released the ball.

But it rolled to a stop before even reaching the first pin.

The crowd let out a groan.

"Should we give the little guy another chance?" asked Bobbi.

The crowd cheered.

The small fry smiled. He took aim and rolled the ball.

"Three pins!" called Bobbi. "That leaves Mr. Clown in the lead."

Now it was Octavia's turn.

A hush went through the crowd.

She took aim and **effortlessly** bowled ...

"Another strike!" called

Bobbi. "This may be a new fair record. **Pick a prize!**"

"I'd like the giant giraffe, please," said Octavia.

The crowd gasped.

The small fry burst into tears and ran off.

"Wait . . . ," Octavia called. "I wanted to . . ."

But the small fry was already gone. Octavia tucked the giraffe into her wagon and sadly slunk away.

"Taking prizes from a child," said a fairgoer.

"What has the fair come to?" muttered another.

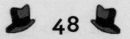

7

The Fun House

As a private eye, it wasn't unusual for Mack to come across some pretty sneaky characters—the Candy Cat Burglars, the Ant Hill Gang, and Skunks McGee, to name a few.

But Octavia Octopus didn't seem to fit the part.

Mack took out his notebook. He reviewed his notes.

"There's something about this case that I'm just not seeing," he said.

"Maybe my photos will help," said Redd. He held up his camera.

Mack and Redd scrolled through the images from the Bowling Game.

They zoomed in. They zoomed out.

In every photo Octavia looked solid and steady.

"I don't see any tricks up her sleeve," said Mack.

"But how is she winning every game?" asked Redd.

Mack was stumped. He was

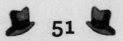

no closer to solving the case.

"Next stop . . . ," he said.

"Report to Al Gator?" asked Redd.

"Soon," said Mack. "First, let's swing by the fun house. I could use a pick-me-up. Plus, it's right on the way to Al's office."

"Yippee!" chirped Redd. **"Follow me!"**

Mack tailed Redd up the ramp and into the fun house.

The first room was filled with wacky mirrors.

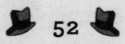

Suddenly Mack was mini!

And Redd was jumbo!

Then Mack was wavy!

And Redd was even wavier!

Mack was feeling better already.

He smiled and walked . . . straight into a mirror.

"This way, Boss," said Redd. "I know this place like the back of my wing."

Redd guided Mack through the mirror maze, across the balance beam, and up the rope ladder.

Redd was solid and steady. It looked like he had been through the fun house a million times before.

"That's it!" cried Mack. "Redd, you're a **genius**!"

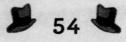

"I am?" asked Redd.

"I just figured out how Octavia is winning every game," said Mack.

"You did?" asked Redd.

But before Mack could explain, the floor beneath them began to **wobble**. It shook. It **shuddered**.

Mack tripped over his funny, floppy shoes. Then he bumped into Redd and they both spilled into the giant spinning barrel.

"Yikes!" hollered Mack.

"Yippee!" squealed Redd.

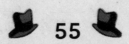 55

The barrel spun them round
and around until they didn't
know which way was up. Then

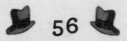

they tumbled out and slid all the way down the super slide and into the safety net.

Whoosh!

"Let's do it again!" said Redd.

"Maybe later," said Mack.

Mack rubbed his head. He rubbed his horn. He even rubbed his red clown nose.

"Oh, I don't like to see a sad clown at the fair," said a kind voice.

Mack looked up.

It was . . . *Octavia?*

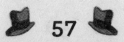 57

She held the glow-in-the-dark space creature out to him. "I hope this brightens your day, Mr. Clown," she said.

A Fairy-Tale Ending

Al Gator rushed over.

"**Mr. Clown!** Mr. Clown," he called. "Are you okay?"

"I couldn't be better," said Mack. Mack took off his round, red nose. He took off his curly, colorful

wig. He took off his funny, floppy shoes.

"Mack Rhino?" Al exclaimed. **"It's you!"**

"Yes, it's me," said Mack. "Mack Rhino, Private Eye. And for cases fair or unfair, I'm your guy. Or . . . rhino."

"Mack and I were undercover," added Redd.

"And it worked," said Al. "I see you've **netted** Octavia Octopus."

"Netted?" asked Octavia. "I'm confused."

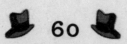

"So were we," said Mack. "This case has been like a fun-house mirror. Things are not as they appear."

"What do you mean?" asked Al.

"I don't think Octavia is trying to spoil the fair at all," explained

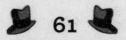

61

Mack. "I think Octavia *loves* the fair."

"That's true!" said Octavia. "I love the rides and games. I love the treats and prizes. It's my favorite time of year."

"Hey, us, too!" chirped Redd.

"But how was she winning every game?" asked Al.

"It took a trip through the fun house with Redd for me to see the answer," Mack said. "This is a simple case of practice makes perfect."

"I do practice a lot," said Octavia

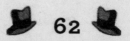

shyly. "In fact, I wish I could be at the fair all year long."

"Is that so?" said Mack. "Al, didn't you mention that you need an extra set of hands around here?"

"I sure do!" said Al with a smile. He turned to Octavia. "How would you like to come work at the Coral Cove Fair?"

"Really?" said Octavia excitedly. "I'd love to."

"Mack Rhino," said Al. "How can I ever thank you?"

 63

"I have an idea," said Octavia. "Mack and Redd will have tickets to the fair every year as our guests!"

"Well, that solves one problem," said Redd, giggling.

Mack took out his notebook. He placed a final check.

Tickets √

Mack Rhino, Private Eye, smiled. He could finally claim the prize on **Case #102—The Unfair Fair Case**—which turned out to be fair enough after all.

"I just have one last question," said Redd.

"What happened to all the prizes?" asked Mack.

"No," said Redd. "Do you think Octavia would join our bowling team?"

Word List

adjusted (uh•JUHS•ted):
Fixed or moved into a better
position

beelined (BEE•lined): Moved in
a quick and direct manner

carousel (care•uh•SELL): A fair
ride with seats, often in the shape
of animals, that goes around a
fixed center

cephalopod (SEF•fuh•luh•pod):
An animal from a category that
includes octopuses and squids

deflated (dee•FLAY•ted): Disappointed

effortlessly (EH•fort•less•lee): Easily; without much work

emerged (ih•MERJD): Came out into view

frustrated (FRUH•stray•ted): Upset or annoyed

genius (JEEN•yuss): A very smart person

glumly (GLUM•lee): Sadly or gloomily

jiffy (JIH•fee): An instant or a split-second

netted (NEH•ted): Caught

shuddered (SHUH•derd): Shivered or shook

to the gills (too thuh GILS): Completely full

ushered (UH•sherd): Led or guided

wobble (WAH•bull): Shake; become unsteady

Questions

1. At the beginning of the story, Mack gets a phone call. Who is calling? What does Mack hear in the background?

2. Why does Al Gator call Mack Rhino for help? Why are the fairgoers getting frustrated?

3. What is Mack and Redd's undercover disguise? Have you ever worn a disguise or costume?

4. How does Mack and Redd's

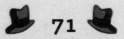 71

trip through the fun house help Mack solve the case?

5. Mack, Redd, and Octavia all love the Coral Cove Fair. It is their favorite time of year. What is your favorite time of year? Why?